Table o

<u>Dedication</u>

This book is dedicated to the dreamers that have been told to give up and do something practical for a career. This is your life. Live it to the fullest and don't ever give up in achieving what others consider impossible.

1

His breath labored, chest heaving as he takes off down a dark alley. The cold night air caressing his fair skin. It's getting harder and harder to breathe with the foul stench of sewage laced in the oxygen he's inhaling. An eerie tune being whistled by his predator as they draw closer to the poor boy. "Haven't you done enough?!" He cries to the assailant, but they're only response is a laugh that sent chills down his spine. His legs are about to give out, but he can't rest. No. Not until he's found safety, which seemed damn-near impossible to him right now. He pants as he continues down the alley. Coming down harder than expected when he steps into a puddle deeper than anticipated by the frightened male. He takes a stumble forward and hits the ground before scrambling to his feet. The scraping of his shoes against the concrete can be heard over the resumed haunting whistle by the hunter.

A chain link fence can be seen ahead and he can't help but curse desperately under his heavy breath. "C'mon, c'mon…" He mutters to himself, gaining whatever confidence he had left in him to use in the attempt to climb the metallic obstacle before him. He grabs onto the thin wiring of the links and frantically pulls himself up as best as he could without losing himself in the process. With one leg now on top, he hops down. Only to slip with his soaked leg and fall back, blacking out when his head hits the concrete.

It was hard to believe that only a few hours ago, he was having the time of his life. Partying the night away with his frat brothers. "Yo, Johnny Boy!" One brother, Lucas, called out to him while making his way through the crowd of people. Dance music blaring throughout the residency being only lit by a mix of strobe lights and several oscillating, multi-colored, disco balls. "Hey!
What's going on?!" John asked when Lucas finally reached him. Doing his best to talk over the music. "I want you to meet my friend Jade!" He replied, tugging a stunning young woman from the crowd. She panted out a sigh of relief from escaping the madness going on in the living room. "Oh, hi!" John spoke, extending his hand toward the girl, "I'm John!" The brunette takes his hand and gives a firm shake before taking her hand back. "Jade! Lovely to meet you!" She responds with a laugh at her attempt to speak louder than the deafening

volume of electronica. Although, her voice is loud enough for him to catch her accent.

"It's nice to meet you too! Where ar-" He was about to ask when Lucas chimed in with the answer to his question. "Jade's from England!!! Isn't that, like, stupid hot?!" He beams and jumps with enthusiasm while she just shakes her head, embarrassed for him. "That's awesome! Where in England?!" John asks.

"London! Have you ever been?!" She replies.

"No, I haven't, yet! But I'm definitely planning on going sometime soon!"

"That's great!"

"Bro! Beer pong!" Lucas shouts and waves John over. Leading him through the crowd and leaving Jade behind. "It was nice talking to you!" She shouts. He just gives a wave and a smile in response, but he swears that he had heard her giggling. Did he have a goofy look or something? Who knows?

After a few intense rounds of beer pong, John drunkenly stumbled onto the dance floor. He busted out moves that he thought were on point, but in reality, were just a mess. Jade eventually found him and they danced for what felt like hours. Laughing and moving, literally dancing the night away. The music was great, Jade was gorgeous, and it was the best night of his entire twenty-five years of life. He was happy.

He wakes up on a bench in the backyard to the sound of a blood-curdling scream coming from inside the house. His vision blurry and his head groggy from the alcohol, he quickly rose from the bench and fell face first onto the grass with a pained groan. When he managed to get to his feet, he headed to the house, rubbing his eyes to see what was going on. It took him a minute to process that the music was no longer playing. Eyes widening in fear at the blood splattered on the windows. "What the fu..?" He whispers to himself, taking a peak through one of the windows. Watching someone stab the source of the screaming multiple times until they fell silent. He couldn't make out the figures through the darkness with only the strobe lights running. But he knew better than to stay put. So, he made a run for it. Yelling out obscenities as he pushed open the gate and dashed out through the front lawn onto the road. That's when he heard a door slam open.

John finally breaks consciousness only to realize that the killer was only a few steps behind him, whistling that menacing tune that will haunt him for the rest of his days; if he were to survive, that is. He fights the headache and gets to his feet before taking off again. Finally getting out of the alleyway and taking a sharp right down the sidewalk. Going as fast as he can on his now wounded leg. The fall did more damage than he realized as he staggered on. The will to survive stronger than ever as he tries to figure out who it was that was hunting him and why.

Did they just crash the party and start killing? Were they already there? Motive? His head was flooded with unanswered questions before the sudden realization that all of his friends were dead. Lucas, Mark, Andre, Wade, Daryll, and the rest of Omega Psi were gone. Tears filled his eyes when he thought of Jade. How scared she must've felt in her last moments and how he wished that he had stayed sober because he could've been there to protect her and possibly save everyone. There was a split-second where he wanted to give up and join his brothers and newfound love in the afterlife, but he knew he had to get word out of what happened before then.

He would've called the police already if he hadn't left his phone in the house. He mentally kicked himself for another moron-move well done. "Yes! Yes!" He exclaims, picking up the pace when a 24-Hour Diner comes into view.

Finally arriving moments later, he bursts through the door and stumbles toward the counter. "Please, I need to use your phone! There's someone after me!" John pleads. The older woman behind the counter, Madge, just rolls her eyes. Kids come in all the time with too much exaggerated nonsense and she just stopped caring after a while. "Relax, kiddo. There's a payphone right over there." She gestures to the other side of the counter on the far side of the diner. "Thank you, thank you!" John races over to the payphone and picks it up. Dialing 9-1-1 then explaining what had happened and giving the dispatcher his location. "Yes, Murphy's Diner. Thank you very much! Hurry!" He hangs up the phone and looks around the diner, finally able to catch his breath.

"Where's your bathroom?" The woman behind the counter points to the door beside him. "Oh! Right…" He clears his throat and goes in. Heading into one of the stalls to do his business as an extra place to hide, should the killer come inside. He's trembling at the thought, trying his best to breathe while he relieves himself. Before exiting the stall, he peeks through the crack to see if anyone was just outside of it. Seeing nothing, he listens out for anything to break the silence. Leaping with fright at the sound of the automatic toilet flushing behind him, "SON OF A— COME ON!" He exhales a breath of relief before going over to the sink to wash his hands. Cleaning off all the dirt and grime before leaning over to splash his face with cold water.

John did his best to scrub his face with a few splashes, too focused on cleaning to realize that someone had walked in. He came back up to wipe the excess water from his eyes and when he opened them, the sight in the mirror caused him to take a sharp breath. Frozen in place, the killer was right behind him. Their face stained with the blood of their victims. His eyes wide as he manages to say his last word. "Jade?"

And that's when I slit his throat.

2

"Oh, darling... You didn't actually think I was even remotely interested, did you?" I smirk, watching him gasp for breath. Blood leaking out from the wound brought on by my special little blade. It was quite fun, really. Being the last thing this man sees before the life leaves his eyes, listening to him gargle and choke on his own blood. "Too bad you have to die, though. You were quite nice." I tilt my head, offering a warm smile that may have come off as cynical to him, "I'd say I'm sorry, but I'm not." Giving a light shrug, I crouch down and press my black-gloved index and middle fingers to the bleeding slice. Making sure I had enough of his crimson lifeline on them before standing up straight. Facing the mirror before using my fingers to write: Viper on the reflecting glass.

Turning back around and leaving him to die on the floor of this disgusting diner. As I exit the bathroom, I notice a man standing just next to the counter observing my last kill before John. He's quite tall. Fat, though. Not pretty one bit. He turns to me and goes wide-eyed like he just put it together. I give a menacing smile before he makes a run for it into the kitchen. "Bloody Hell…" I huff, chasing after him. Only to be met with a butcher knife being swung at my face as soon as I get through the door. "You're gonna pay for what you did to Madge!" He yells as I back up against the wall, ducking at his latest swing, and swiftly move behind him with a quick slice to his side. He's awfully big and it's going to take more than just my knife to take him down. While he's tending to his wound and shouting in pain, I look around for something to use against him. Smirking when I find a lovely frying pan on the stove. Taking a hold of the handle, I turn it over with the intent of hitting him with the hot end of the tool.

He takes another swing with his hulking butcher knife, but my cut makes him less accurate and I manage to shield myself with the frying pan. Reaching out to stab at him a few times while he's recuperating. Looking as if his last swing really took a lot out of him, I take advantage of the situation and drive the frying pan right into his fat, ugly, face. He cried out in pain and stumbled back against the counter where I then pounced and gave one last powerful strike right to the temple. It didn't knock him out like I'd hoped, but it did give me enough time to thrust my blade into his jugular. His blood spurting out all over my face and dress as he fell. Squealing with joy at the fresh shower of warm, red, liquid. "Have a good night, love." I beam as I crouch down, stabbing him repeatedly in the heart to make sure he was dead.

After the lovely kitchen fight, I head back out and over to break into the cash register. Pocketing all the cash and smacking the bottom to make it rain change everywhere. Wanting a bigger mess for whoever has to clean this up. Then I look around for the office to destroy the security footage. Once the system is smashed to bits, I hear the sirens and quickly make my exit, heading into a side street away from the flashing lights.

It didn't take *too* long to get home. Only about an hour or so, but when I did, my roommate started screaming at me for what I did. She knew I was the killer because she was the reason I started killing in the first place. My best friend from college, Jennifer Scott. I just rolled my eyes at her and pushed my way to the kitchen for a bottle of water from the fridge. "What were you thinking?! Again?! Come on, Jade! You're better than this!" She lectures as I take a sip of water. "You bloody well know I can't control it! Sod off." I glare at her and she backs down. "Well, you're on the news again. The infamous Viper… Why'd you pick that name, anyway?" She asks.

I give a small shrug and take another sip of my water. "Sounded cool. I'm going to shower and get

these sodding people off of me. Movie after?" I ask.
She nods, "Sure."

3

I let the hot water wash over me. The dried blood coming off with the pressure of the showerhead, closing my eyes to enjoy the soothing heat of the stream while they hit my natural form. I wasn't always a killer. No. I was actually an average student in university studying to get my law degree. It wasn't until my third year that my dark side had surfaced. This addiction, this insatiable need to take a life, the darkest thing I could possibly become. It's the thing of nightmares. Quite strange, really. I want to stop the bodies from piling, but I just have this burning hunger that craves the blood, screams, and the sight of the life leaving a victim's eyes. It sickens, yet at the same time, arouses me to the point where I just continue to give in to the darkness.

It started when Jen came into the dorm 6 years ago. She gushed about this frat party at the Delta Nu house because Ricardo Lopez had invited her to go and I remember how in love with him she was. It was kind of adorable, so, how could I possibly say no to going and be her wingman? We went and it was a pretty spectacular night. I wore my tight pink party dress and she wore her slutty black dress. She called it her "sex dress" because it's easy to get off and looks hot.

"Jaaadddeee!!!" Jen whined, pulling me aside into the hallway. "Sasha keeps going all over Ricardo and I can't even freakin' get any face time in…" I'm too drunk at this point to fully understand what she's saying, so, I say the words I've come to regret later that night and every day since. "Then why don't you flirt with Matt and just make Ricardo jealous?"

Took about an hour or so of flirting with him and jealous exchanging of looks. Oddly enough, she actually went upstairs with Matt. A little far for my taste, but who am I to judge? I kept on dancing until I got tired and decided I wanted to go home. But, I couldn't leave without my roommate because she's the one that usually woke me up for class in the morning with her alarm. "Where did that sodding crumpet go?" I ask myself as I search throughout the house as well as the back and front yards. Nowhere to be found until I went upstairs to hear screaming over the overwhelming sounds of people talking and music blasting. "JEN!?" I call out to her. All I hear her say is, "Help." And I fling open the door to find Matt has her tied up on the bed in mid-rape.

Then everything went red. In a blind rage, I grab the first thing I see from the dresser beside the door, which is an empty beer bottle and I let loose with a fearsome cry. Smashing the bottle over his head before he could even pull out. The glass shattered, and that wasn't enough. I began stabbing and cutting, slashing until I was covered in blood splatter and the light completely left his eyes. But I didn't stop there. No. I was angry that I was the *only* one to do anything. The only one that heard her cry for help and stepped in to save her.

I'll be damned if I didn't make them all pay for what they were too bloody cowardly to do. That was when I snapped and the darkness came loose. I let Jen go home before I went downstairs, gathered the outside party goers in, and locked all the doors and windows. Watching them all partying as if nothing had even happened, then, I took to the kitchen and picked up the biggest knife I could handle. My vision was completely red as I slit the throat of the first guest I found, but nobody was sober enough to realize what I had just done was real. I stabbed the next one in the heart and kicked them down.

Took five kills in total for party-wide panic to ensue. But everything was locked… I slaughtered them all like animals. It was an utter gore-fest for the horror fans to get off on. A blood bath for the ages, and when it was all over, I stood in the middle of the living room with the music still playing and I danced to the music still blaring over the speakers. The word viper being whispered through the beats, and I realized that I had just found my calling. I wrote it on the front door in my victims' blood, with gloves on, of course. Then, I took to getting my fingerprints off of the knife as well as the broken bottle upstairs, sporting the lovely yellow rubber gloves from beneath the sink; taking them with me to dispose of later. As I got rid of the evidence leading to me being the killer, I realized how much I enjoyed this. The killing. The rush of getting rid of damning evidence that could lock me away for the rest of my life.

I enjoyed it, so much so, that I started to scare myself. Who had I become? *What* had I become? A bloody monster. This is not what I wanted, this isn't the life I had planned out for myself. I wanted to be a top-notch lawyer, head of my very own firm somewhere in the States. Instead, I was this... I became... *this*. This, this, this... EVIL! I hated myself, hated this new me. Jade Two-Point-NO, if you will. But at the same time... It was devilishly arousing. Exciting me to my very core and changing my heart from this bright light with a successful future, to a dark shadow of my former self. Yes, if I get away with this massacre, I could go on and still be the lawyer I had set out to be. Kill for sport while locking up the ones stupid enough to get caught. Who am I? I'm horrified by these thoughts, cursed thoughts that I just want to go away. I fight and I fight, but they fight back harder. The door had been opened and I lost the key to lock it again. It was too late, though. Darkness was here and already taking over. I could either fight and lose, or just give in and be free.

The next day, it was all over the news and the rumors spread around campus like wildfire. Headlines in the newspaper and online articles spelled out one name. The name that will forever belong to the darkness that I have become. Viper.

Then came the interviews. Everyone who was known to be at the party or thought to be going to the party was a suspect in what was now known to be the "Viper Slayings". I actually found the name to be quite amusing and the article even better than the headline suggests. Told of some students spotted leaving the premises of the Delta Nu house with the murder weapon. "Idiots." I thought aloud to myself with the hint of a smirk. Jen was up next while the interviewees waited outside the Dean's Office.

"I'm nervous…" She spoke, her eyes to the floor. I shook my head, pulling her into my arms. "Shhh, darling. You didn't do anything wrong." I say, giving her an assuring squeeze. "Still…" She looks around then whispers in my ear, "I know you did it." Releasing a soft sigh, I lightly comb my fingers through her soft blonde hair. "You know nothing, love. I took you home after the *incident* with Matt and stayed with you until we both fell asleep in our dorm." She nods.

Rising when the Dean's secretary called her in after releasing the previous student.

It was about ten to fifteen minutes before Jen came out, she was crying, hopefully more over the bloodbath than ratting me out. She barely even looked at me as she walked out the door, but I think I got a hint of a thumbs-up. Big wave of relief crashing over me at the threat of being caught and thrown in prison for the rest of my life being gone. Phew.

My interview, however, was interesting. The Dean and the Detective in charge of the interview both acted like I did it, but at the same time knew I was innocent. I wanted to smirk, but I refused to let it show. Any sign of suspicion could throw up a red flag. Of course the harsh interrogation was all just for show. They think a man did it according to false witness accounts. As if a girl like me could possibly have done such a horrible thing. It was nice to know that I already had the upper hand. Lovely.

"I didn't see anyone that I didn't already know from class, sir. All I know is my best friend was raped at that party and I just needed to get her home in a safe place. I was planning on going down to the Police Station with her the morning after, but by the time I had already woken up, the story was all over the news." I started to tear up as if I were actually upset about the situation. The Dean offered me a tissue. "Don't worry, Miss Cross. We'll get to the bottom of it and get Miss Scott the justice she deserves." He waved me off as I took the tissue. "Thank you… Please find the man, Officer. It's hard to feel safe in class with a killer loose on the grounds." The Detective gave a nod, told me that the police were doing their best in the investigation, and let the Viper go back to her dorm.

4

After the incident at Delta Nu, Jen didn't want to
pursue a law degree anymore. Instead, she switched
her major to business and knocked law down to her
minor. Now she owns a strip club downtown called:
Our Little Secret. It's the most exclusive club in the
entire city and she really looks out for the girls like
I looked out for her that night. Waivers need to be
signed before you get in and background checks are
required if the customer would like a private room.
There's security at every corner of the building. It
really is quite the place. I help with the most of the
legal things that she's too busy to deal with and she
swoops in with the assist on cases that she can offer
her expertise in. Jennifer is the best friend a serial
killer could ever ask for.

I wake up the next morning after movie night with
Jen, and get ready for work. Ignoring the news
about the Viper striking again at a local diner.
Knowing it would only cause another potential
argument between Jen and me. We've talked about

it loads of times before and that's why she automatically shut down when I told her that I couldn't control it. She knows that killing is like a drug to me and how hard I try to kick the addiction, but the darkness always has a way of coming out. I've stayed away from drinking and drugs for the most part, out of fear that I would lose myself and just give in to the Viper without a fight. It was *always* a fight. The back and forth battle of my mind raging in my head like an indecisive war between choosing two vacations you desperately want to go on. Listing pros and cons, compromising every little bit just to make a choice. It's insufferable.

Honestly, I don't know how I manage to make it out of bed in the morning. Maybe it's because I need a distraction from my own thoughts, attempting to drown the Viper with useless, day-to-day obligations and such. Who knows?

After getting dressed, I head off to the firm of Locke, Quinn, Jackson, and Cross. Handing off a bag containing a breakfast sandwich to the receptionist, Ava, from her favorite place in town, Cat's. I've done that every morning since I got to know her, plus, it was on my route to work, so, it's quite convenient as well. There's just something warm about brightening someone's day by doing the smallest thing. It always seems to do the trick when it comes to the fight against Viper, gives me the upper hand, but after that? Leaves me vulnerable to attack while I'm doing my victory dance since I have no other moves from there aside from the usual.

Being a lawyer doesn't help, either. When it comes to reviewing the cases; Viper always steps in with some hard hits, especially when it comes to murder cases. She never misses with those ones. Coming up with ideas for ways to not get caught, figuring out where the killer went wrong and making a note of it for when I take my next life. It's heartbreaking.

While her winning those battles is a disadvantage to my state of mind, it turns around and becomes my winning strategy in the courtroom. Proving my clients innocent by laying out the groundwork for how the event took place, stating how they couldn't possibly have done it. But, if I was being honest… It wasn't me winning those cases. It was Viper. The darkness inside of me coming out in the courtroom, doing whatever she possibly can to cover up the crimes and make the guilty party innocent when there was seemingly no chance of being able to do so.

She twists around the words of the Plaintiff, turning the evidence in favor for the Defendant's case rather than against them. It's quite poetic, really. Almost like an out of body experience, watching myself command the courtroom, ruling as if the Judge had no choice but to grant me the winner every time. The Viper had yet to lose a case and I couldn't help but feel proud, yet, horrified to know that the evil that dwelled in my head was letting the other demons go free without giving any kind of justice for the victims of these trials. I've tried to step down, just quit the firm, but, she would always stop me a split second beforehand. Taking over in my moment of hesitation.

This is not the life I wanted for myself. Putting innocents away by day and murdering them by night. Yet, still – Every day I wake up and go through it day by day, waiting for the inevitable end of my being. It's a miracle that I haven't been caught, yet. Feels as though I would never be released from this prison I call life. Perhaps this is my punishment for all the evil I've done the past few years.

5

The following morning; beams of warmth peeked through the slivers of my bedroom window's blinds. Brightness shining through lidded eyes rouses me just moments before my alarm performs the single task it has been given the previous night. I hit the snooze button to steal a few extra minutes of relaxation for the day ahead. The craving to be refreshed and ready to take on the routine waiting for me when I awaken, motivates my short return to dreamland; the one place I feel truly safe from the Viper's persuasion.

I'm ready to go as the alarm sounds off. Killing the noise with a flick of the switch as I rise out of bed and head straight for the closet; snatching a plain-white blouse followed by a gray blazer, with a matching pair of pants in the top drawer of my dresser. They rest comfortably above my delicates, while my socks sit just below them at the very bottom.

Once dressed in the appropriate professional attire for a lawyer such as myself, I pull my brunette strands back into a tight bun, clipping my bangs neatly to the side. "Perfect." I mutter aloud to no one; glancing over myself in the mirror to approve of the outfit before making the necessary adjustments for a better appearance. When that was all over, I begin my artwork on the blank canvass that is my darling face. Taking about twenty or so minutes to get it done. Now I was ready to officially start my day by heading to Cat's for breakfast. I felt the need to get something different than my usual order today. Yearning for a whole-wheat bagel with cream cheese and a large hot chocolate with extra mini-marshmallows. Yum! Little did I know what the morning had in store for me.

Upon receiving my order, I take a seat at the booth by the window to enjoy my meal; something I never do, but it was a gorgeous day outside and I wanted to soak it all in. The sun's rays warm my features through the pane of glass while I take a small bite out of my bagel. I can't help but close my eyes as the sensation of serenity washed over me. It had been a long time since I've felt like this. So relaxed. I even smile to myself. Today is a good day.

But, alas, my trance had been broken by an erratic woman causing a scene in the middle of the establishment. Screaming about how the service is too slow and ridiculous people making such complicated orders when all she wanted was her coffee so she could get to work. Angered brown eyes fly open to glare at the reddened monstrosity that ruined my moment of peace. She had the poor barista, Joshua, cowering in fear while he tries his best to get her to calm down whilst trembling uncontrollably. I cracked my mouth just a sliver, about to stand up to the woman, but Viper shut my lips and kept me still. "Soon…" She whispers. We had just found our next victim.

I calmly finish my bagel as a bystander while the episode unfolds before me. The manager stepping in to fulfill the woman's wishes, well, *demands* really. My eyes follow her while she storms out of the building and I rise out of my seat as the door closes, making my way to the counter to drop a five-hundred dollar tip into the jar with a wink to Joshua. His face lights up at the gesture. "Don't lose your faith, love." And with that, I exit through the door, hot chocolate in hand. I'm out just in time to catch the woman getting into a taxi, hailing my own and telling the driver to follow.

We're trailing them for a good few miles, weaving through the city until she finally stops at the SJB Marketing Company building. "So, this is where you work." I whisper, a devilish smirk tugging at the corner of my lips. I ask the driver to pull ahead and drop me off around the corner as to not raise any suspicion of being followed.

Once out of the car, I pay the driver and leave him a healthy tip before making my way over to the courtyard of the building. Not wanting to go inside just yet, but to survey the area and figure out the best way to pick the pocket of my prey later on to get more information on her. Taking a seat at the water fountain, I breathe in the fresh morning air and enjoy the rest of my hot chocolate. After a moment or so of peace, I check the time on my phone: 8:15a.m.; then call my secretary to let him know I would be coming in late today. I have a much more pressing matter that requires my attention.

Around twenty minutes go by before I decide to leave my post and survey the inside of my victim's place of work. The interior of the structure is incredibly spacious and inviting, yet, intimidating at the same time. It's quite exciting and I end up with a bright grin on my face as I look around; which is nothing compared to the sunlight flooding in from the multiple windows surrounding the perimeter of the property. "Absolutely lovely." I say to myself. Brown eyes rapidly moving through every inch of the place to try and take it all in. An island desk rests in the middle of the lobby with the space inside being occupied by three employees; two sporting security uniforms and the third looking rather dressed up with a headset resting comfortably on his left ear, the receptionist.

As I arrive to Reception, I manage to catch the young man's nametag while he, Daniel, slips on his best customer service face. "Hi! How can I help you today?"

"Terribly sorry to bother you, but, I was just wondering if I could possibly use your restroom?" My foreign accent evident and clear, knowing the British tongue soothes and fascinates Americans. "It just makes you sound all smart and proper." My friends would tell me.

"Of course!" Daniel responds. His smile seeming more genuine and relaxed this time around, "It is right down that hall and to your left. Can't miss it."

"Thank you so much." I show my gratitude with a sweet smile of my own before making my way to the bathroom; not that I actually had to go. I just needed an excuse to survey the premises so I wasn't looking as if I were just wandering around without permission. The brilliant architecture of the place made it almost *too* easy to act like a tourist and look as if I were simply admiring the modern design when in reality I was tracking my prey, searching for any sign of her with unfortunately no luck. I wasn't in there long, but, just enough time to erase suspicion of any kind from my being there. Thanking the concierge on the way out, I check the time. 8:45 a.m. Just enough time to get Ava's daily coffee order from Cat's, where they tried to show their gratitude for my generosity by offering the beverage on the house, but I insisted on paying. Businesses needs money to run, and that tip is to be used for something that makes them enjoy their lives; a reminder that the world isn't all bad.

Upon my arrival to the firm, I manage to schedule lunch slightly earlier today, needing to go back to SJB Marketing for more surveillance in the hopes of catching this woman either leaving or returning from her second meal of the day. The pre-requisites for the kill are to know when she gets on and off of her break, where she goes for it, if anywhere, and when her work day ends. Always best to know your prey in order to pinpoint the exact time to strike and how to approach the attack when it's time. It's hunting season, and the Viper is out for blood.

6

As much as I'd like to do nothing but plan out the kill, I've got real work to do to sustain my way of life. Although sorting through case files wasn't glamourous, it was fun to pick which clients to represent. I usually go with the one I find to be the most interesting, in fact, there's a murder suit that just manages to catch my eye: James Robert Dawson charged for the murder of his 16 year old son, Nathaniel. "Interesting." I mutter to myself as I continue my investigation. There's solid evidence, witness accounts seem accurate, but of course, he pleads 'Not Guilty'. Well, I can certainly see why. Christian family man heavily involved with the church must be killing his reputation to be accused of such an atrocity. I suppose if he were a true man of God, that he'd be facing his demons head-on and deal with the consequences of his own actions rather than push the darkness aside in order to be seen as the clean, well-rounded, God-fearing productive member of society that he appears to be. But, you know the saying. Takes one to know one.

I press down on the intercom button to page my secretary, Brandon, and let him know to make the necessary arrangements for the Dawson trial. He's guilty, of course, but it's money in my pocket when I convince the jury of his faux-innocence. Besides, he's next on Viper's hit list after she-who-is-yet-to-be-named. "Got it, boss." Brandon responds. I thank him, then, go back to building the case to prove his plea. Sifting through the crime scene photos, reading over the eyewitness testimonies, I prepare my arguments against the plaintiff.

Hours go by and as I'm writing out my notes that will turn the evidence against my client to work in his favor, the beep of the intercom sounds off, followed by Brandon's voice. "Sorry to bother you, Miss Cross, but, Amelia Dawson is here to see you." The series of loud noises breaking the silence startled me enough to have me at least an inch off my desk chair. I start laughing it off, nodding as if he can see me, "Bloody Hell, you frightened me." "Sorry again, boss. Shall I send her in?" He asks. Again, I nod, wondering why I'm behaving like a bobble head. "Yes, send her in. Thank you, Brandon."

I'm in the middle of organizing my desk when she walks in. Taken back a bit by how much more attractive she is in person than in the photographs on my desk, but she's thankfully too worried about her unannounced visit to notice the surprise in my expression. "I'm sorry for just showing up like this without an appointment, but, I just wanted to thank you in person for taking my husband's case." She says. I give her a warm smile as I rise from my seat. "No worries, love. I was actually just working on it. Please, have a seat." I move out from behind the desk to formally greet her with a firm handshake. "Amelia, is it?" The woman nods. "Jade Cross. Pleasure." I grin and am met with a grateful smile in return. "The pleasure is all mine, I assure you." She replies, "Thank you, again, for seeing me. I know I should have waited to make an appointment, but I was just so excited that someone actually took us on."

"Yes, well, the evidence against your husband is quite circumstantial, but, I'm confident that I'll be able to convince the judge and jury otherwise. Get him home where he belongs." I tell her. "Then six-feet under." The Viper's whisper echoes through my head. I shushed her.

"You have no idea how much that means to me." Amelia chokes out, the joy in her eyes evident as she's happy to see someone willing to fight for her broken nuclear family. "So many lawyers have either turned us away or just wanted to take a plea deal because they believe he's guilty. But... James wouldn't do something like that, especially not to his own son... Our baby boy..." She starts to lose control of her emotions when it comes to her – I check the file – first born child. Tears crawling down her face. It saddens me to see her this way.

"Hey, hey. Shhh…" I whisper gently; snatching the box of tissues from my desk before moving beside her. Offering the box with a soothing caress of her upper back. She leans into it, accepting the comfort being given by her lawyer, and using the tissues to calm herself down enough to a controlled level before fixing herself back up. "It'll be alright, love. I've been doing my research and I can honestly say that I believe in your husband's innocence and I will do whatever it takes to keep him out of prison." I lie for the most part. He is obviously guilty, but, I will win this case. It's what I do. "I won't rest until James is free and your son's true killer is brought to justice. You have my word."

7

It is finally time for lunch and I need to draw any type of potential suspicion away from my activities. Which means, no deviating *too* much from my usual midday routine aside from it being earlier than normal. I stop by Lucia's Tacos, the food truck that's always parked outside of the firm, because the area is teeming with high-paid professionals that love authentic food. Today, though, I take my order with me to the workplace currently employing my prey, hoping to bump into her and finally get a name. It should be her lunch hour as well.

Releasing a soft sigh of relief as I arrive just in time to spot her exiting another taxi. Lady Luck is certainly on my side with this one. I pull my phone out from my pocket, mime-texting as my cover for not paying attention when I *accidentally* bump into her; casually removing the wallet from her designer purse and inconspicuously slip it into my pocket. "I am so sorry!" I say, doing my best impression of a clueless American girl, apologizing to her multiple times. But, with her being the short-tempered woman that she is, told me to buzz off in her own colorful version of the English language. Oh, darling… that's going to cost extra.

My eyes trail her while she goes inside, not-so-subtly mumbling profanities under her breath as she does so, before I continue on my path around the block in order to take a proper gander at the contents of her wallet. Reading over information on the driver's license. "Well, Stephanie Annabelle King of 401 Hemlock Drive, it's lovely to meet you."

8

Now powered by the knowledge I required in order to better prep my next victim for the end of their life, I am able to organize my life with more efficiency; holding off on the strike until James Dawson's case is closed. I didn't take too long to compose my defense, only a few days or so to get it just right. Choosing the proper jury, however, was much more time consuming until it was finally time to deliver my opening statement in front of the entire courtroom. "Ladies and gentlemen of the jury. We are here today because of a boy. A boy who was taken away from his loving, happy, and beautiful family in the most disturbing and horrific of ways you can only begin to imagine. Nathaniel Clark Dawson is dead because someone didn't value how incredibly precious his life was and what it could turn into. Such a devastating loss to the world to lose one of its brightest stars. He was on the debate team, you know. So incredibly smart and athletically talented, excelling both on the field and in the classroom. We have truly lost an exceptional human being and I mourn his death and share in the suffering of his family."

As I continue, I move out from my position behind the podium to command the room and captivate the attention of my audience. "What's worse is that his father, James Robert Dawson, is being falsely accused of committing this heinous act on his own first-born son! James and Amelia Dawson deserve to the time to grieve the catastrophic loss of their first-born child, who is survived by his darling 10 year old sister, Nora. Yet, James is being falsely accused of murdering his own flesh and blood... I just find it so hard to believe that the plaintiff has the audacity to do such a thing to a man clearly in mourning. A man who is suffering and in such incredible pain over the death of his son."

I pause for a slow exhale as if I'm trying to keep my emotions under control, turning my head back with sad, sympathetic eyes to James in the seat beside mine; Amelia behind him on the opposite side of the barrier. She comforts a tearful Nora as silence falls over the courtroom. I look around at each and every person in the room, appearing to be at a loss for words. Closing my eyes and taking another deep breath, I maintain the silence for another moment and a half for dramatic effect before finally speaking. "James Dawson is good man. A wholesome, righteous, God-fearing, Christian man that goes to church every single Sunday to serve and inspire people to better their daily lives through their faith. I have met him. I have talked with him. This man wouldn't hurt a fly, much less murder his own son."

I go on to deliver quite the performance, one of my best, I would say. In the end, the Viper had twisted every word against James around, causing all evidence against him to be null and void. All witness testimonies torn apart with a fiery passion as if I actually cared for this vile, putrid, disgusting excuse of a man. James Robert Dawson is truly guilty for killing his son, but Viper was sure to see that the jury voted otherwise. "Not guilty." The lead juror states when asked the verdict by the judge. Case won. Viper's hiss echoes through my head entangled with glee at yet another victory for our practice.

9

The following day, Amelia shows up at my office, unannounced, yet again; this time to thank me for doing my job correctly. I never understood why I was ever thanked for winning cases. For one thing, I'm taking your money; for another, that's my job, it's what I have to do or else I'd have to find another career. With all that money and time spent on university? I don't bloody think so. "You really don't have to do that, love, but I do appreciate your gratitude." I respond, slightly annoyed at her presence.

"Nonsense! How I was raised, if anyone does anything good for you, you thank them. Whether they had to do it or not. It's just the polite thing to do." She smiles.

"Well, thank you. That's very sweet." I tell her, trying to be brief.

"Of course! Oh, and I didn't come here to just thank you. I also wanted to invite you to dinner at our house, so, we can all thank you together." She offers, and I want to protest, but the look in her eyes makes it hard to say no. Besides, she's living with her son's killer and I can't just let my next victim free to kill again. Especially, when the next kill could be this darling butterfly and the precious dove she's got waiting for her. "I know Nora would be so happy if you could make it."

There it was, she pulled the cute little girl card and I would be considered a real monster if I disappointed that sweet child by rejecting her offer. This woman knows how to sell; tugging on my heartstrings using her daughter like that. I end up shaking my head, throwing my hands in playful defeat. "When you put it that way, I have no choice, do I?" My laughter brings out her own and we just smile at each other for a moment. Her persistence to get me to dinner was wildly attractive; wearing me down like she did. I can't help but get curious over the mystery that is Amelia Dawson.

After the details for the dinner were all sorted out, it was time to find something to wear. I can't wear something too casual such as denim and a t-shirt. A dress might be too formal, depending on the type of dress, but that particular one is not yet included in my wardrobe. Why was I worrying so much, though? It's just a family dinner. Not like I'm meeting the parents of my romantic interest. It's a dinner honoring me for what I've done for them. That's all.

41

I ultimately decide on a simple white button-up with a light grey cardigan, matching knee-length skirt over black leggings. Should be fine, right? I look over my outfit of choice in the mirror, nodding in approval as I check on every angle. Stepping into a pair of black ballet flats to complete the ensemble, I'm out the door and on my way to supper.

I arrive at the Dawson residence a few minutes early, fortunately. Giving me enough time to breathe, questioning why I'm so nervous. I pull down the mirror above me and fix myself up to look presentable. Heart pounding in my chest and I can't stop myself from groaning aloud. "Why am I so damn nervous? It's just dinner with a nice family!" I yell at myself in the mirror. If anyone were to walk by, they would probably want to send me off to the psyche ward, and my career would be over as I know it. "Because he's guilty!!" Viper responds with a snarl from the back of my mind. I narrow my eyes in the mirror, "I will *NOT* kill him!" I spit back the venom in her face with a grimace. "At least…" She responds quietly while I take a glance over at the house, peering inside as I'm able to see them setting up the meal in what I assume is the dining room, "…not yet."

Once I was inside and got all of the greetings out of the way, Amelia takes me on a tour of the house while James and Nora finish setting the table. The home is exactly what you would expect from a

Christian household. Various types of scripture painted on the walls, crosses hung on the chimney with care, clean, but very well decorated. The Dawson's have exquisite taste, and overall the place is quite lovely. Feels like a home. Comfortable.

Amelia tells me the stories of how everything got decorated, where the ideas sprung, and when they bought everything. It was nice to hear about her life, I could listen to her talk for hours. Her voice is so… calming. Makes me happy to know that someone like her exists in this world. Among the stories, though, she lets me in on a secret of hers, leaning in close. "I actually built some of this stuff, put them together myself." She whispers with a soft giggle, "I love doing those types of things, but James doesn't like it. He believes that the man should be doing the handy-work and the woman doing the three C's. Cooking, cleaning, caring." As she goes on about his ways and her home life, I can hear the Viper's hiss echoing through my head. He'll get his… Oh, darling, don't you worry… He'll get his.

When the tour was over, it is finally time to eat. The scent of steak, mashed potatoes, creamed corn, salad, and warm, sliced Italian bread with butter baked in hit my nose like a ton of bricks. My mouth watering at the restaurant-esque dinner that they had prepared. It all looked incredible appetizing and I can't remember the last time I had a home-cooked family meal like this. The aroma of each dish

43

floating in the air, mixing together, and creating a heavenly fragrance that I simply could not get enough of.

I was about to start eating, going as far as to pierce my steak with the tines of my fork, when I notice they start taking each other's hands. Glancing between James' and Nora's hands reaching for mine. "Oh!" I laugh softly before setting my utensils down to join hands and complete the circle. Following along with their family tradition of saying grace before starting on their food. My eyes respectfully close while I listen to James lead the prayer; hearing him thanking God for bringing me into their lives and saving him from his – well deserved – prison sentence. I notice how he doesn't mention the fact that he is supposedly innocent for the crime. Oh, my dear James. You will be truly confessing your sins soon enough.

When all was said and done, amens recited, I could feel Amelia's gaze while I finally started to eat the savory steak before me. "Are you a believer, Jade?" She questions with genuine curiosity. My eyes rotate from my plate to meet hers, heading tilting slightly to the side while I ponder the answer to her question. "No, not really, I suppose. I believe in getting things done myself rather than asking someone up above to do it for me as a favor that I could never really repay. With that being said, I do, however, believe that there could very well be such a thing as God, seeing as there's all this evidence to support His existence. But, I'm one of those people that has to personally see it to really believe it, you know?"

Amelia smiles at my answer, understanding exactly where I am coming from. She's about to respond, lips parting, when James cuts her off. That strikes a nerve with me. "Well, how about you come to church with us tomorrow morning? You might find that something you need to believe." Nora chimes in excitedly, "Yeah!" She looks up my way from her seat, I can't help but beam at how utterly adorable she is. "Will you come, Jade? Pretty please?!" She's bouncing now and her parents are laughing at their 10 year old's persistence. Just like her mother, she knew how to play the cute-kid card. "How can I possibly say no to you, little dove?" I laugh, "Of course I'll go." "Are you sure?" Amelia asks from the opposite side of the table. "You don't have to if you really don't want to."

"She just said she will." James steps in, stating the obvious. I want to glare at him, I really do, but now is not the time.

"No, no." I wave dismissively with a small laugh, "I want to go. Honest."

Amelia's face lights up immediately, and I can feel my smile widening with the corners of my lips tugging as far apart as they can go. "Truthfully, I didn't have plans, anyway. Just going to sit in my bedroom in my jammies and binge on Netflix and junk food. So, it all works out."

We spend the rest of the evening swapping memories of our lives, the adventures we've been on, and they even shared bits of Nathaniel's life with me. It was lovely to know the person whose death I would be avenging soon. They told me the tale of how they met at the arcade when they were young. She was playing some game that I didn't bother remembering the name of and he had asked if he could be her Player 2. Their love sort of blossomed since and it was adorable how they wove the story together. My story of why I became a lawyer only paled in comparison to it, especially considering that I'm still single. Not that I was really looking for a romantic partner. My life at the moment didn't have enough room for that sort of thing and I'm okay with it. The right person will come at the right time and I truly have faith that it will be magical endeavor.

10

Early the next morning, I arrive at the church with the address provided by the lovely Amelia. A breath of relief escaping my lungs when I see her standing in front of the establishment, waiting patiently for my arrival. I'm out of the car, engine silenced, waving to my new friend as I make my way over to her. She races to meet me with an enthusiastic embrace when I'm finally caught in her sights. I return the gesture of affection before she leads me into the building, through the lobby, and into the main room where James and Nora were seated and waiting for us. "Jade!" Nora exclaims, getting up from her spot to throw her arms around my waist when I'm close enough. "Oomph!" I grunt, giggling softly as I hug her back firmly. "It's nice to see you too, little dove." I stroke her hair when I let go and follow her back to her spot on the bench. Amelia occupying the space on the other side of me. Strange how she doesn't want to sit next to her husband, but, is it? Does she know the truth?

The service starts when a youthful rock group takes the stage in the front of the room. They perform songs about how great God is and what He's done for them with both literal and metaphorical lyrics portraying their love for Him. The band was entertaining to say the least. Regular attendees rising from their seats and lifting their hands as people would normally do at concerts in praise for the source of their favorite music. However, this scene looks a bit different. It's as if they are surrendering themselves... Strange. I've never seen anything like that before in a religious institution.

When the performance was over, the Pastor comes out, silently instructing the band to soften the instrumentals for dramatic effect while she speaks. The notion piques my interest and I lean forward to pay attention. She introduces herself as Pastor Rachel Pierce and begins her sermon by reading a designated passage from the Bible. The scripture John 8:44 appears on the screens set up on either side of the stage where the lyrics to the songs were once displayed. "Your father is the devil," She starts, "and you do exactly what he wants. He has always been a murderer and a liar. There is nothing truthful about him..." She goes on, but I'm suddenly unable to focus on her words. Why can't I pay attention? I blink a few times, narrowing my eyes as I try to get a read on the situation at hand.

Murderer and liar. Murderer and liar. Murderer and liar – MURDERER AND LIAR!!! The phrase screams in repetition through my ears, but it's not coming from Pastor Rachel. What in sodding hell is going on!? MURDERER AND LIAR. The phrase gets louder and louder in my head until it reaches a deafening decibel. "Viper."

The hiss of the darkness within me kills the words of John. She watches its literary essence pour out over the floor and drain into the bottomless abyss that is my mind. Then, like the flip of a switch, she takes over and projects a vision before me that wipes out the reality of the room. She's in control now and can show me what she damn well pleases.

I watch on as the entirety of the congregation fades to a massacre. Bodies thrown all over the room and I'm unable to move from my seat. I'm paralyzed and all I can do is sit there and watch in horror at the scene. Pools of crimson flood the area as the liquid drains from their hosts. Why am I seeing this? Why can't I move? Why am I so bloody powerless in my own head?! I want to scream, but the sound is sealed tight in my throat and the only thing escaping is the air from my lungs. My hands ball into fists, eyes hot with tears staining my features as I'm forced to look on. It is truly a bloodbath for the ages.

My brown eyes manage to focus on the stage as a mysterious figure appears over the lifeless body of Pastor Rachel. The figure's back is turned toward me and all I can see is the knife in their hand soiled by the blood of their victims. Their head whips around and my expression widens with fear as I'm now trembling in place when I see exactly who it is. Me. Blood drips down from her form and we suddenly lock eyes. The red-stained version of myself smirks. "Viper…" She whispers.

The lights flicker and I'm no longer sitting down. I find myself standing in the middle aisle surrounded by bodies. The Dawsons are laid out in front of me. Dismembered. Their sawed limbs spelling out the dreaded word: V I P E R.

"NO!" I finally manage to let the sound out, screaming the word at the top of my lungs as vision unfolds. Tears streaming like a waterfall down my cheeks and my eyes shutting tight. I feel a hand on my shoulder and my eyelids fly open from the chill running down my spine at the fear of who the hand might belong to. Only to find that the horror was gone and the church had gone back to normal. Well, *almost* normal. The room had gone so silent you could hear a pin drop onto heavy carpet. All eyes are on me with both a concerned and terrified expression. I realize how badly I'm shaking and try forcing myself to stop, finding that the hand on my shoulder belongs to Amelia. My tear-stained eyes meeting hers that mirror everyone else's.

"What's wrong, Jade?" She asks in a deeply worried tone.

"I... I've got to go." I barely get the words out before I perform the action. I go. Storming out of the building, I'm still violently trembling as I rummage through my pockets for my car keys. Hardly able to hold it together when I get to my vehicle. Hands uncontrollable as I open the door and frantically fumble around to get the key in the ignition to start the car. Peeling out of the parking lot, I just drive in the direction of home. The only place where I could feel safe and free from the Viper's spell. This wasn't the first time a vision like that had happened, and I doubt it would be the last, but this is the first time it had affected me so badly. I couldn't for the life of me figure out why. My breath is heavy, heart racing and pounding in my chest, finding it harder and harder to get back in control of my own body. "FUCK!" I slam on the wheel, swerving out of the way of an oncoming car before I pull over and kill the engine on the side of the road. Then, I cry.

11

It was a while before I finally responded to one of Amelia's multiple phone calls. The woman was relentless, but, I'm glad she respected my feelings enough to not show up uninvited to the office this time. Just made me admire her further. "Yes, yes. I'm fine, love. I'm just going through a lot right now that I would rather not talk about at the moment." I tell her. "Oh, okay. Well, I'll keep praying for you!" She says as chipper as she can sound over the phone.

"Thank you, Amelia. I appreciate your kindness, but it's really not necessary…" I trail off with a soft sigh.

She obviously heard my exhale through the speaker. "Maybe we can get lunch or something soon? Just hang out?" She says.

I simply shake my head as if she can see me. "I don't know."

"Please?" She persists, desperate in her need to find out what had happened at church. Probably thinking that she was the problem, that maybe she did or said something that triggered the reaction.

I take a deep breath, using my free hand to lightly massage my closed eyelids. "Alright, Amelia..." I say, "We'll go to lunch. I'm free on Thursday if that's good for you."

"That's perfect!" She smiles, I know she does. I can just tell by the way she said the words.

I return it with something small of my own, a soft chuckle, and we continue the conversation with empty small talk before we hang up.

I don't know what I'm doing. I don't want to see her or anybody else for that matter. Especially after that ghastly incident. I can't remember the last time one of Viper's visions were that frightening. It was probably the first one, I had no idea what was happening then. All I remember was being at my cousin's wedding in Wales and I just lost it. I was paralyzed and couldn't do anything about it. Just had to watch myself slaughtering my entire family like they meant absolutely nothing to me. When it was finally over, I ran to the lake and just collapsed. Sobbing uncontrollably and I prayed that it wasn't real. Fortunately, it wasn't. It was more of a *day*mare, I realized.

The visions after that were certainly gruesome, but, I honestly didn't care as much as the first time and even the more recent one in the church. Honestly, I haven't the slightest idea about why I cared so much. It might be because I haven't been given a vision like that in a while, maybe it was Viper's way of checking-in. Perhaps I was just getting too close to the family? To tell you the truth, I haven't kept anyone close to me, except Jen; the only one who knows who I really am and what I've done since that night at the Delta Nu house all those years ago.

The only reason, I suspect, Viper has allowed me to keep her alive is because, in a way, Jen is like her mother. Having given birth to the venomous creature that dwells within my mind by being a victim of a crime that shouldn't have happened. I am but a vessel for her to reside in and use as she pleases, only keeping me and her mother alive. It's ironic, considering that if Matt had finished the job, she might actually be a mother to a demon spawn. Thankfully, I killed him before he could, yet... here we are.

I'm a murderer barely in control of my own mind and body, quenching the Viper's thirst whenever she sees fit, and the most I can do was help her be smart about her kills to avoid getting caught in the green mile to trek. What a wonderful life I lead.

"So, what are you gonna talk about?" Jennifer asks while she occupies the empty space on the couch beside me, wielding a freshly brewed mug of tea. "I have absolutely no idea." I let out a soft sigh, whining a bit as I give her a look, silently screaming for her to help me. "She's probably going to preach some scripture to me that she believes pertains to my situation or something."

"She could... but, you never know. It could actually be geared exactly to what you're going through with Viper. I mean, like, have you seen what those people can do? It's like they have a sixth sense sometimes. It's scary as hell." She chuckles.

"Oh, yeah?" I lead, raising a single eyebrow at her. "Like what?"

"Okay, like, just the other day. A group of these born-again women came out to the club to talk to the girls with absolutely no judgments, only wanting to help them lead better lives, ya know?" She starts, I'm nodding, intrigued by what she's saying. "Go on." "Yeah, this one lady goes over to Cindy and starts to ask her all of these questions about her life. Mind you, these are all completely dead-on questions that you would never dream of actually having to do with some stranger's life. I'm telling you that she *KNEW* these things, it's crazy. Anyway, then she starts saying all this stuff that God knows what she's going through and is looking out for her and all this awesome stuff. Brought the poor girl to tears. I even talked to her about it after she said that it was all true down to the tiniest little detail! It was insane."

She gave me a lot to think about when it came to my lunch with Amelia, like, how I shouldn't go in there assuming that she was just going to preach to me when she could possibly be there as a concerned friend and nothing more. I do have to come up with a cover story, however, for my little scene at the church, but it's no big deal. I'm sure I can whip something up. Definitely not going to tell her about Viper anytime soon, if not, ever. That would not end well at all. I'd either be on the run or in jail, but I would dragging her sodding husband down with me. See how she likes that.

12

Thursday finally came and we decided to meet at the location of my most recent slayings for lunch. Murphy's Diner. While the police may suspect the killer would return to the scene of the crime, they're still under the impression that the Viper is male. Perfect cover for a lady such as myself.

Upon my arrival, I notice a banner hanging beneath the giant sign giving the name of the eatery. "Under new management? Whoops." I bite my bottom lip as I make my way inside. Finding that Amelia was already seated in a booth by the window on the left side of the room. She held what I assume to be a cup of coffee in her hands. Her face lighting up when she catches me in her sights. "Jade! You made it."

"Hello, Amelia." I smile and take the seat opposite of her in the booth. "Have you been waiting long?"

She shakes her head. "No, not really. Only been about ten minutes." She smiles, "Sorry, I got here a little earlier than we planned. Was a little excited." She giggles. I check my watch and she's right. Five minutes to one. I was a little early too.

"Oh! Did you finish errands early or were you just happy to see me?" I tease, giving a playful smirk.

"A little bit of both, actually." She plays along, nodding her head. We both end up laughing together

I order something simple when the waiter finds his way to us. Hot chocolate and a turkey sandwich on whole wheat. My conversation with Amelia starts out slow. Mostly small talk about the weather, work, current events, Nora, et cetera. Then the awkward silence hits for a few moments and I take the time to glance out the window at the day going on. Clouds hovering above, looks as if it's going to rain.

Amelia clears her throat and starts to speak up, much to my dismay. I knew it was coming, but I was just holding out hope that it was never going to be brought up. Letting out a soft sigh, I remember the excuse for my behavior at the church. It should be a good enough reason, especially, if I tell it right. "So, what happened at church?" She asks with puppy dog eyes, and I
hate that it's working. I'm afraid to answer right away and take a sip of my hot chocolate for an extra moment of silent bliss before I answer her. Inhaling

a deep breath, I finally speak. "Have you heard of the Viper?" She nods, leaning over the table with clear intrigue over her features.

"Yes, well, I was there at the beginning… for his first slaying at that frat house. I had just barely missed it with my roommate, Jen. Luckily she wasn't feeling very well and I took her back to our dorm. Then morning came and we heard the news… I guess it's just become somewhat of a survivor's guilt mixed with P.T.S.D? I don't know. But, I see him sometimes. He's only a shadow, but at the church, it felt like he was in the room with us." I clear my throat, blinking back a few tears as I fight away the memory.

"Silly, I know, but what I saw… I just…" My voice cracks and I'm unable to fight it back anymore. Tears are falling and I drop my face in my palms, elbows anchoring my arms down on the table.

"Hey, hey…" Amelia says with that calming voice of hers. It's like being wrapped up in a warm blanket. She takes one of my hands, using her thumb to gently massage the back. Empathy in her eyes. "You're okay, Jade. It's okay. You're safe here… He can't hurt you." She says in an effort to get me to relax, and, thankfully, it works. She hands me a napkin to use as a tissue using her free hand. I wipe my eyes before accepting the kind gesture from the woman, reluctantly pulling my hand from her grip to blow my nose into the cheap paper; fixing myself up.

"Sorry about that." I sniff and set the napkin aside with an empty laugh, clearing my throat.

"Don't worry about it, hon. It's not your fault. I shouldn't have pried." She says with her bottom lip poking out slightly. She's right for the most part, wrong for the others. It is my fault. "There are some things that happen in this life we are given that we just can't control no matter how hard we try, and when that happens, we lose it. We shove it all down deep and try our best to forget about it, but it never works because it all just festers below the surface and it always finds a way out no matter what you do. The best thing we can do is face it head on, accept the fact that we have no control, and go from there." She says.

I'm trying to understand what she meant, and some of it is processing, but none of it fits together like it should. "So, the way that we control these things, you're saying, is to not control it?" I ask, confused. "Exactly." She nods. "You can't control the event, but you can control the outcome based on how you handle the event when it happens. Face the shadow, stop fighting him, and accept what he's done as a part of who you are now. That's how you win."

Her words hit right at home, but strikes a nerve with the Viper. She definitely did not like that Amelia basically just gave me instructions on how to take my life back from her. Huh... Jen was right, after all. But her being right is a small victory compared to what Viper has in store for the near-future, planning out her next kill to be as ruthless as she possibly can as a scare tactic to try and stop me from listening to Amelia. The King family isn't going to know what hit them.

13

It had been about two weeks since my lunch with
Amelia. Viper had taken over for the most part,
spending the better part of my days plotting the
King Family Massacre. She had me running by the
King home every day; making it part of my daily
routine. I would park a few blocks away and go,
stopping every once in a while in front of the house
for a water break. I would watch Mr.
King play with the children in the yard, a young boy
and girl around Nora's age. It was interesting to see
that Mr. King is a stay-at-home dad, considering the
norm where the women are usually at home being
the primary parent while the father is out at work,
making the money to support their livelihood.
Lovely to see that it wasn't the case here, though.
It's a shame they're all going to die soon.

The rest of the neighborhood was clean, however.
As in, no security cameras in view of the home and
no nosy neighbors close enough to the residence to
care. Well, none that could see in the dark, anyway.
The best part about it, though? They never lock
their doors. Nice enough neighborhood gives them a

false sense of security. That won't last much longer. I'll make sure of that. Viper's hiss of satisfaction of our investigation rings through my ear canals. "Tomorrow…" She whispers. I nod and stretch my legs, taking another swig from my water bottle. "Tomorrow." I reply quietly under my breath. One more glance into the yard to find Mr. King waving to his killer as a friendly gesture of hello. The Viper waves back to her prey with a genuine smile of maniacal joy. "He has no idea what's coming for him." Her words like silk running through my fingertips. "None of them do."

The following night, I pull my brunette hair back into a high ponytail; sporting a dark red sweater, black yoga pants with knives sheathed in a sleek black belt, and black gloves to avoid any fingerprints; armed with brass-knuckle blades – my go-to weapon of choice – throwing daggers, and double-edged ring knives. Slipping on a sling-bag filled with rope, smelling salts, handcuffs, and a nine millimeter handgun with attached silencer just in case things go south and they need to be quick kills.

When it's time, I take my usual route to the King home, parking in the same spot three blocks away before I run. Noticing very few lights were on in the neighborhood, always a good sign. I vault the fence into the yard and inconspicuously make my way to the sliding glass door in the back; staying out of the light shining from the living room and kitchen. Upon reaching the door, I pin myself against the wall beside it to stay in the dark while I wait for whomever is in the kitchen to leave, so, I can make my entry. Getting into position for me to look between the window and the door to watch for shadows moving around, trying to pinpoint an exact location for the suspect.

Once it was finally clear for me to make my way inside without detection, I pull the door open just enough for me to slip through before closing it behind me. Taking shelter behind the island counter. "Move!" Viper barks at me, but I shake my head. It wasn't time, yet. We have to be smart about this because there's a million ways this could all go wrong and I need to take a hostage to secure my plan and make sure things go my way. I look to either side of the island, waiting to find a shadow making its way over, checking the reflection in the kitchen window to see which direction the owner is facing before making my move. "NOW!" Viper screams in my ear, adrenaline rushing through my veins giving me the fuel I need to get behind my first victim.

Stephanie herself. Slinging an arm around her shoulders, I press a brass-knuckle blade to her throat and whisper in her ear, "Don't scream, darling. It'll only make things worse for your lovely little family in there." I smirk, "Move." The order comes stern out of my mouth as I nudge her forward to the living room where the rest of her family awaits their missing member. "Honey…" The woman speaks to get her husband's attention on my command. "Ye-? Oh!" His eyes widen in shock at the sight of my knife securely pinned against his lover's neck, ready to cut at a moment's notice. "Wh-who are you? What d-do you want?" He asks, obvious fear in his voice, just how I like it. The son and daughter cower behind their father in fear when the reality of the situation hits processes in their developing brains.

"Shhh, love. No questions or she dies." I extend my elbow out in a threatening manner, acting as if I were about to slice. He nods in response and wraps his arms around the children. "Nice to meet the King clan formally." I grin devilishly, "You. Husband." I say as I unclip the bag from my back and toss it at him. "There's rope in there. Do me a favor and tie the children up, won't you?" The man moves as if he's about to try something, but I only push the stainless steel harder to his wife's throat. The blade getting a small taste of her scarlet life from the light cut. "Wouldn't do that if I were you, hubby." I tell him.

He swallows the lump in his throat, understanding now that he needs to do what I say or suffer the consequences of his actions against me. I watch him work on tying the children's hands and feet together as directed by his stunning captor; then proceeds to tie his own feet together when I tell him to. "Such a good listener. Where did you find him, Steph? I've got to get me one of those." I tease and I can feel her tense up at the mention of her name. "Ah, yes. I know your name. More on that later. For now, tie his hands together." I kick her over to him, knife to her spine for motivation while she knots his wrists with the rope provided by yours truly.

"Okay, King family!" I exclaim with a menacing grin. Moving the knife away from Stephanie's back to deliver a swift punch to the temple. I watch as her unconscious body drops to the floor, listening to the cries of terror from her kids. "Don't worry, children. Mummy's not dead. Just knocked out." I reassure them before duct-taping their mouths shut, doing the same to their dear old dad. I tie up the resting woman while she's out and set her in formation with the rest of her lineage.

"So, King family… Who is ready for story time?" I giggle with a clap of my hands, "This one is quite good, I assure you. It's a lovely tale about how your wife," I point to the man before pointing to the children, "and your mother pissed off the Viper." I smirk, watching their level of fear increase. "I know, right? Viper is supposed to be a big scary man, not some attractive daffodil from England. It's funny what the media can come up with that's so far from the truth and how many people believe it.

Anyway, now you know the truth. Shame, though, that none of you will live to tell the tale."

Their tears, trembling, and sheer look of terror in their eyes brings me such satisfaction and I know I'm doing a bloody damn good job at this. Viper is pleased, but, I want to make it last a little longer. Wait for little Miss Let-Me-Speak-To-Your-Manager over there to wake up. Always a good thing to be prepared with the smelling salts to control when she wakes up, learned that the hard way. Now, I'm in control of when this vile woman awakens to see her family slaughtered right before her very eyes. Until then, her bloodline at least deserved to know why they are going to die tonight.

"So, you see, I was getting breakfast on a lovely Tuesday morning at my favorite spot in the city. Then, all of a sudden, this manic woman bursts through the doors, going completely mental. She's screaming and demanding service, causing quite the scene because this poor minimum wage working lad wasn't moving fast enough with the other patient customers during his morning shift with far less co-workers than he needed that day. Absolutely ruined my day and drove the boy to tears! And for what? A cup of coffee?! Madness, I tell you! Cost me a few hundred dollars in the tip jar of my own money to bring a little happiness to his day, make him smile, and restore his faith in the goodness of humanity." I tell them, weaving the tale of how their short-tempered oaf of a matriarch got them killed as a consequence for her unnecessary actions in the coffee shop that day.

"Ironic, right? A serial killer wanting to restore someone's faith in humanity. It's funny." I smile, looking at them as if I were expecting either of them to laugh. "Well, anyway. You have your mum to thank for this when you get to the good place." I shrug and pull out one of the smelling salts from my pack, popping it open before putting it to the unconscious female's nostrils. She wakes up violently, thrashing about while she throws a coughing fit so ferocious I thought she might kill herself.

"Good morning, sunshine." I grin, patting her cheek to keep her awake as well as to let her know that this is reality. "I was just telling your lovely family all about your disgusting display of proper coffee shop etiquette at Cat's a few weeks ago. You've pissed off the Viper, love. Not smart. But, congratulations on killing your family." I chuckle, grabbing her husband by the hair to drag him out in front of his genealogy. "So, I'm going to call you Simon. You look like a Simon, is that alright?" He nods frantically in response as if it would free him from death.

"Lovely! Alright, Simon. So. I have recently been to church and am incredibly enlightened now. There's this thing that gets you a free ticket into Heaven, did you know this? It's called the salvation prayer. Now, since you've done nothing wrong, I'm going to ask you to say it with me."

I can hear him whining behind the tape as he struggles to get free, but I back-hand him across the face to shut him up. "Giving you a free pass, darling. Don't mess it up, now." Clearing my throat, I being. "Repeat after me… Dear, God. I beg your forgiveness, for, I repent for my sins. I believe you died on the cross for me, I believe you are the one true father. I ask that you come into my heart and make me new." I listen to him repeating every muffled word behind the tape, and finally, as soon as he's finished with saying amen, I make a clean cut around his neck in the shape of a smile. Tugging his head back to make the blood flood out from the wound, watching as some of the liquid spritz out onto the rest of the King clan. I can't help but laugh at all the mess, throwing the body to the floor to let it bleed out over the carpeting.

"So, who's next?" I smirk, listening to the screams dulled by duct tape. "Is it going to be little Timmy? Or sweet Sally?" I ask, twisting my lips to the side as if I really knew their names. Only name I needed to know was Stephanie's. "Timmy it is! Ladies last, huh?" I throw Sally a playful wink. "One for the girls." I drag the boy over through the pool of blood coating the floor over to his father's corpse, pondering where to stick the knife when we were doing going through the whole prayer thing again. He deserved the good place as well, not his fault his mother's a raging twat. "Say goodbye to mummy." I decide to drive the steel straight through the back of his left side to penetrate the heart. Waiting for the light to leave his eyes as his mother watches before I drop the lifeless sack by its creator.

Finally, last but not least of the undeserving is the eldest of the two children. Sweet little Sally… I decide to make her death a quick one as she reminds me of Nora, the little dove that had stolen my heart. Her mother was a sweet one, but James… Oh, no. He deserves a much worse fate than having Amelia and his second child killed in front of him, he'd probably prefer to do the honors himself, the vile man. I spit in the blood puddle in front of me after reciting the prayer with the child before forcing my blade directly through her soft skull into the brain. Barely able to fight back the tear that fell from my eye when I watch the life leave hers.

Viper sending another vision through my head of darling little Nora dying in my arms by my hand instead of this Jane Doe child. I manage to break the spell because she wants me to finish the kill, kicking Sally's body down beside her brother's to get the knife out of her head. That was just a tad more effort than I wanted to use, but, what are you going to do? I shrug as I make my way over to the first domino that started the chain of events leading to her family's demise. "Do you see what you've done? You see the error of your ways, don't you? This isn't my doing, oh, no, darling. This is all YOU! You disgusting waste of human life. If you were just a little more patient and understanding and much, much, less angry with the world, your family would be alive right now and you all would be enjoying a nice evening in." I scold her and tear off the duct tape.

"Do you have anything to say for yourself?" I ask, lifting an eyebrow.

She's about to apologize, but she doesn't deserve the chance to finish those words. My knife punctures through her forehead before she could utter her last words, mouth now free to do so. "That's what you get for wasting your pathetic excuse for a life on cruelty."

I have to kick her down as well, with much more elbow grease than I needed for her daughter for obvious reasons. As soon as the thud of the body hits the blood-soaked floor, another sound rings throughout the house; high-pitched squealing. My eyes widen in fear. "No... No, no, no, no..." I dart straight toward the source of the noise, making my way through the maze of the house before I finally come across the nursery. Finding the baby screaming their little lungs out in the crib. From the decorations, I'm able to confidently determine that the infant is a boy, no need for a diaper check. I look over the crib to watch him squirming in there, wondering where his mother is and when she's going to feed him or change him. Tears start to fall and my heart drops as I consider my options on what I should do.

Then… silence.

Once it was made known that this particular slashing was the Viper's doing, I clean up and rig the scene as if a man had done it before going home. Racing out to my car with everything I had brought with me, I drove away as if I had just finished my run, no need to be hasty with my commute home because that only raises suspicion and you never know who could be watching.

When I was finally home, I stripped out of my Viper outfit and threw every article in the laundry for cleaning while I hopped into the bathroom for a quick shower. Anxiously awaiting the usual amazing dream that lay ahead of me after a satisfying kill. Viper's way of showing her appreciation for a job well done. "Murderer and liar! Murderer and liar!" The phrase rings through my mind again once I'm dressed for bed and nestled under the sheets. Brown eyes widening when I realized what was coming. "….Viper."

"NO!" I was back at the church, surrounded by bloodshed. What's going on!? VIPER! I want the dream that I deserve! I shout to her, but there's no response. Not even a hiss. All I can see are the bodies... there are so many bodies. They're coated in the substance that once gave them life. I fight back my tears, taking a deep breath, and tell myself that this isn't real. It's just a dream, it's not real. Then, I blink.

Blood-stained corpses now directly in my personal space, surrounding me. Their clouded eyes all staring at me and I feel my heart sink down to my stomach, my stomach dropping further into nothing until all I'm left with is standing there in pain. Suffering like my victims had suffered. "Murderer and liar!" They all started chanting. "Murder and liar! Murderer! Murderer!"

A knife appears in my palm and I squeeze the handle, closing my eyes, releasing a slow shaky breath. About to fight my way through the seemingly endless sea of casualties, but, when I open my eyes, they are all gone. All that's left of them is the sea of blood taking up the entirety of the room. I use this time as a chance to escape, throwing open the doors that I had hoped would lead to my freedom, only to be met with the frat party at Delta Nu. The soiree that started it all. "No, no, no, no, no..." I shake my head, looking around at all the faces, frantically searching for Jen's in the crowd and praying to God that she's okay right now.

The music cuts out and in a flash of the strobe light, every party-goer is turned around. All eyes on me. Every flicker of the strobe light transforming their appearance to look as dead as I had left them all those years ago. The cuts, stab wounds, bits and pieces of their bodies strewn over the floor. A girl screams in terror, "You killed us!" And, in an instant, their reddened carcasses have me backed into a corner chanting loudly in unison. "Viper! Viper! Viper!" My back to the wall, I slide down to the blood-soaked floor and drop the knife I had been holding as I pull my knees to my chest and start bawling. "I'm sorry!!!" I cry out, but they're as relentless as I was to them. Who I am being an endless chorus turning back on me. "Viper! Viper! Viper!"

The room is spinning and I close my eyes, desperately fighting to feel the sheets of my bed under my fingertips stained with the life essence of my first victims. "Come on! Come on!" I scream, but it's no use. This is my new reality and I have to accept it. Once I come to the realization, I finally wake up. Drops of salty discharge streaming down my face as I pant heavily. Scanning my bedroom for anything out of the ordinary, thankfully, nothing is. I'm safe in my own room. But, am I? I come to the conclusion that I need to stop fighting my shadow self, accept her as part of who I am, and take control of her. No longer killing for her, and taking my life back by starving Viper until she dies. "No. More. Blood." I whisper to myself. No more death will be caused by these hands ever again.

14

5 years later…

"Mom! Mom! Mom!" The sound of my five year old son's voice manages to find its way into my bedroom, echoing throughout the vicinity, and startling me awake. "Oh, sodding– What?!" I call back to him, fumbling my way out of bed. "I'm hungry!" He cries. "Alright, alright. Mummy's coming, love!" I yawn and stretch out before getting dressed in simple loungewear, not needing to go to work for another hour or so. Stepping into my slippers, I make my way downstairs as he demands that I hurry up. Normally, I would scold him for talking to me in such a manner, but, he was right. I woke up late today and I can't help the roll of my eyes at the nonsense of my parenting method. My mother would've bloody beaten the life out of me if I talked to her like that, but, I digress.

Making my way into the kitchen, I find him seated atop one of the stools at the counter, waiting quite impatiently to be served. "Alright, Xander. Relax." I tell him calmly as I start making breakfast. "You do know you have a sister to demand these tedious tasks of, right?" I ask him, raising an eyebrow in his direction. "I know, but I like your cooking way better." He replies and it's ugh. So sweet. I can hardly stop myself from kissing his precious face, ignoring his disapproval of my smothering him before I start on breakfast. Whipping up a simple meal consisting of scrambled eggs, toast, sausage, and bacon for my lovely adopted son and sleepy step-daughter that is just now making her way over to join her brother and myself. My partner-in-crime had already left for work, unfortunately, so, no family breakfast.

"Hey, J?" The fifteen year old girl speaks up, setting her phone aside.

"Yes, little dove?" I ask in return while I'm whisking the eggs in a bowl.

She bites her lip nervously, fear in her eyes for what's to come after she says what's on her mind. "What do you do when you like a boy?"

"Oh." I'm taken aback by her question, pausing and doing a few blinks to process the surprising information. Well, I guess it shouldn't be surprising since she is a teenager now, but I suppose it's surprising in the sense that she's asking me about it. "Um, well… Why don't you explain the situation, love? I can help you better once I have all the facts." I give her a warm smile before sending Xander into the living room, telling him I'd call him once breakfast was ready.

She starts opening up when her brother is out of earshot, elaborating more on what's going on in her life while I continue with breakfast. She tells me how handsome she thinks this boy is and how she feels when she's around him. It's quite an adorable story, but, unfortunately as she goes on, it all starts to crumble when she says that he doesn't really pay much attention to her when she talks. Only really listening when they're in some spirited debate about some rubbish I don't bother remembering.

"He sounds like a waste of time, little dove. You deserve so much better than what he's giving you." I tell her straight out, not wanting to beat around the bush with a subject matter like this.
"You deserve someone who looks at you like you are their entire world. Someone who finds beauty in your flaws, and adores the sound of your voice, Nora. You have such a lovely voice that needs to be admired by someone who appreciates every word that travels upon it."

Once breakfast was ready, I call Xander in to enjoy the feast with three-fourths of his family before I got ready for work and take both children to their individual schools on the way to the firm; now officially called Jackson, Quinn, Danvers, and Cross. We had to let Locke go because they weren't really a team player.

"Mrs. Cross?" My new assistant, Winter, speaks over the intercom in my office. "Amelia is here to see you."

"Send her in." I reply with the push of a button.

"Right away."

When the com unit closes out for the last time, I rise out of my seat and move from behind the desk to happily greet my wife with a gentle kiss and warm embrace as she walks through the door. "You left early this morning." I say, taking the to-go bag from Cat's she had brought for my lunch.

"Yeah, I'm sorry, sweetie." There she goes with the apologies again, the darling butterfly. "Jen called me in to Our Little Secret to help her fix some accounting problem with Ivy's last paycheck." My wife explains, casually making her way over to slip her arms around my waist; my own moving to drape over her shoulders.

"Oh, right! I forgot that she quit. I'm glad she finally graduated from Uni." I smile up into Amelia's soft eyes. "So, guess who has a crush on a boy?" I tease, watching her eyes go wide as her face lights up; gasping in surprise.

"Really?! She finally told you?!"

"She did!"

"Well, spit it out! Who is it?!" Amelia questions with excitement laced in her voice, poking at my sides playfully to get me to squirm and confess what I know.

"Oh, just some wanker that she's too good for." I shrug. "He hardly gives her the time of day and they apparently fight a lot as barely even friends. Doesn't notice her otherwise, so... waste of time."

She nods, crinkling her nose in disgust at what I've told her. "Well, damn. Why does she like him, then?"

"Hell if I know, darling. But, I do know that there will be other, much better, boys worthy of her affections." I tell her with a bright smile. She mirrors it ten-fold and I can't stop myself from melting into her comforting arms. I love her so much.

The rest of the more-than-welcome visit to my place of work, we talked about Xander not really fitting in with the rest of his classmates and how much it was affecting me, unsure what to do about the situation. Was I bad mother? Am I raising him wrong? I sigh, but Amelia assures me that he's only five and still has plenty of time to come out of his shell. "He will, soon. I promise." She tells me, "Nora was the same way when she was his age, and now look at her." This fact made me smile, after everything we've been through, that little dove had spread her wings and started to fly so gracefully.

After I had completed my eight hours for the day, I went home and am greeted by a multitude of affection from Nora, Xander, and especially from the lovely Amelia Cross; who, by the way, had dinner already prepared for us to appreciate as a family in the living room while we watch our shows. Another normal night in with the ones I love.

15

This normal life didn't come without its challenges, though. Falling in love, getting married, and raising two children were definitely not on my list of plans I had made for myself half a decade ago. Still, I wouldn't trade it for the world. I cherish every memory, every decision, every single moment I have been through since the horrendous nightmare that scared me straight. It's shaped me into the hardworking lawyer and mother I am today with no bloodshed whatsoever. Viper was dead and I finally have my life back.

I guess the biggest change came about four years ago. Amelia had called me one night; hysterical, crying, and screaming at James in the background. I could hear him threatening poor
Nora and that's the moment I decided it was time to step in; driving directly over and phoning the police along the way. Now, I wasn't one to call the police for assistance in a situation as dire as this, but I had given up killing and they were around the best option I had. Especially, since I had planned to take

him to trial for the murder of Nathaniel on the opposing side this time. I'm sure I have Amelia's blessing to do so.

When I arrive to the house, I could see James attacking his wife through the dining room window. "No!" I cry out as if they could possibly hear me from my car. Rage building the explosive fire that now controls my actions as I kick in the door and jump in to save Amelia from any certain death if he had continued to beat her the way that he did. I had tackled him off of her, his strength outmatched mine while we wrestled around, fighting for dominance. Nora's screams for her mother ringing throughout the house, adding to the struggle of the fight.

James may have had the advantage when it came to power, but my cunning and training for this very thing gave me the ability to come out on top. Delivering a powerful blow to his throat and another to the waste of space between his legs while he attempted to choke me out, ultimately failing. While he caught his breath, writhing in pain, I used the opportunity to throw a firm punch to his temple enough to lose consciousness. Then I go over to Amelia's battered frame, stroking her hair while she tried to do her best to stay awake. "Nora!" I call out to my little dove, "It's alright. Daddy can't hurt you anymore, I promise." My breathing was heavy from battle, but I did everything I could to keep talking to

Amelia in a valiant effort to keep her awake so the severe concussion wouldn't drive her into a coma.

The police finally arrive shortly after Nora makes her way over to her mother and I. James just barely waking. I gave my statement while they put the bastard in the back of a squad car, Amelia hardly able to talk enough to give her statement that they would eventually take when she's recovered in the hospital. Nora had stayed with Jen and I until Amelia was discharged and that's where our love story truly began.

We had already been dating a few weeks when James' trial came around and I managed to make things right by sending him to prison for Nathaniel's murder and the attempted murder of his wife and daughter. Another month or so after that, I came to the conclusion that I wanted a child of my own to raise. Having the incredible support of both Amelia and Nora. Nora excited to have a brother or sister, but, our relationship wasn't quite there yet. I took Xander in since nobody else wanted him because of the bad mojo of his past that came with him. His family was murdered, by me, about a year and a half prior. Poor lad. I had to or else the guilt of him growing up in a bad home and becoming a copycat killer would weigh down on me over the years. At least he'd having a fighting chance to make something more of himself with me.

Amelia proposed the following year with a much too public display at the firm. She managed to book my favorite band, Blackout, to come into the office and perform an acoustic rendition of our song. All the while, she spoke into the microphone. "Jade Allison Cross... I don't know where to begin telling you how I feel about you." She starts, "You have saved me so many times in more ways than one. Starting with the first time I just showed up here to your job unannounced because you so graciously accepted the case against my jerk of an ex-husband, but,

I'm not here to talk about him today. I want to talk about you. How you rescued me and my sweet baby girl from him like our very own guardian angel. It doesn't help that you look like one, am I right, guys?" She coaxes my co-workers into agreeing with her and they all erupt with laughter. Some recording the best moment of my life on their phones that I would ask them to send to me afterward.

She goes on to list all of the reasons why she fell in love with me and how much I mean to her. Thanking me for taking Nora in when she was in no way my responsibility while she was recovering in the hospital. Then finally, the music swelled, fading out as she sunk down to one knee and asked me to be hers for the rest of our lives. You can probably guess my answer by the way things turned out. I have been undeniably happy ever since and nothing could possibly change that, well, almost nothing. There was still the tiniest sliver of a chance that Viper could make her return and take over completely now that my walls were down and I was seemingly unprepared for a battle. But, I assure you, I am ready to win that fight.

16

Unfortunately, I don't believe that this happy life of mine isn't going to last much longer. I've been good for so long… aren't I due for a relapse? I'm in the kitchen hand-washing the dishes after our Saturday afternoon family lunch. "Hey, J?" Nora makes her presence known with my nickname. Amelia is her mother and always will be, and to be honest, I actually prefer that my parental name is a single letter, but only to Nora. Xander is sure to face my wrath if he dared call me that. Besides, Nora still sees me as an equal authority figure to her mum and I'm happy with that. It's also an adorable thing that's just between us. Helps us bond.

"Yes, love?" I respond as I turn off the faucet, setting the clean dish I had been working on into the drying rack. My eyes meet hers and the worry on her face is troubling. What's going on? I think to myself, not knowing what to expect. I begin to wonder if that boy she told me about did anything to her during one of their 'debates' and started to get furious, having half a mind to go to his house and sue the bloody pants off of the family if he harmed her in any way. My darling little dove.

"It's Xander…" She finally gets out and my train of thought arrives at the station of emptiness as my heart freefalls into my stomach. He knows, doesn't he? How did he find out? I was sure to keep his past a secret from him, build up his parents into an extraordinary fantasy and they couldn't keep him because they were too busy saving the world from monsters out to hurt him. That's why he can't make any friends… I sigh, giving a slight shake of the head. I guess it was bound to come out sooner or later. Let's get this over with. "What's the matter with Xander?" I ask her. She furrows her brows. "He, um… told me something that was a little disturbing…" Nora shakes her head, fighting to get the words out but it's obvious that it's hard for her to say.

What could it possibly be? What could he have told her? She's getting choked up and my eyes catch a few tear drops as they fall down her cheeks. Well, now I'm really scared. A multitude of scenarios fly through my head, but I have to be the strong one. She needs comforting right now, you're the parent. I tell myself as I move over to pull her into a tight hug. "Shhh, little dove. I'll talk to him myself, okay? Just go get your mum for me, then listen to some music or something.

Distract yourself because whatever it is, it's not your job to handle it. Go be a kid and don't grow up too fast." I tell her with a gentle press of my lips to her forehead. She sniffs with a light nod, wiping her eyes dry. "We'll talk soon, I promise."

I watch her leave the room to get Amelia like I told her to, trying to throw the horrible scenarios out of my head while I go to Xander's bedroom to get to the bottom of the situation. The door's nearly completely open and I watch him play with his toys for a moment, admiring the innocence and joy before whatever is going to happen unfolds. I knock on the door before I get too caught up in the moment. "Come in." He says, looking over to see who did the knocking and the brightest smile appeared on his face at the sight of me. "Hello, my sweet boy." I greet him in a gentle tone, taking the empty space on the floor beside him; resting on my knees. "So, your sister started to tell me the story you told her, but something came up and she didn't get to really tell me anything." I laugh softly, even though I was dying inside. "Well, that's rude of her." He tells me and the giggle that escapes me is genuine from his adorable tone. "Exactly. So, how about you tell me? I'd love to hear it." I smile warmly and reach over to comb my fingers through his light hair. He just went back to playing with his toys, not really ignoring me, but just to preoccupy himself to settle his shyness enough to tell me this epic fable as I often did when I was his age. Must be a phase.

Then he started to unravel the tale of the boy and Mr. Wilson, who, just so happens to be his teacher. Xander told of their adventures in the boys' bathroom at school when he had to go use the potty and how uncomfortable he got with the 'extra' help he had received from the teacher. The fury burns through the entirety of my body as I listen on, forcing myself to remain calm in front of him as to not make it seem like he did anything wrong. My eyes find Amelia's shadow as she's standing in the door way, listening in as well. I can't look at her, because if I look at her, I'll cry and if I cry, Xander will feel like it's his fault. Can't have my sweet boy thinking he did anything wrong. He's doing the right thing by telling me and I'll be sure that he knows that once this is all over.

He goes on with the rest of the story that I tried to ignore, sugar-coating the narrative in my head. Telling me about things he's had to do for extra credit on some assignment. "Kill him!" The familiar hiss sends a jolt of electricity down my spine and I'm frozen in place, stricken with fear as I realized what this means. It had been so long since the Viper's voice echoed throughout my head. I had hoped to God that she was dead, but, clearly my wishes aren't part of his 'divine plan'. The rubbish. Although, the might have actually been gone, and hearing the unspeakable acts to my son must have resuscitated her. Either way, she is back and I doubt she's going away without a fight.

"No! I will *NOT* spill any more blood for you!" The shouting match begins in my head between us, doing my best to resist her influence. The pervert will pay for his crimes by being thrown in prison to rot with Nora's father. Justice will be served the *right* way, not her way. Oh, but she was having none of it. She's starved long enough and will do whatever it takes to live.

This is about Viper's survival now. What does a snake do when they're backed into a corner? They strike with every last drop of venom in their system to ensure their victory. Then her latest vision hits and I'm powerless to stop it from projecting before me. "This is my mind!" I shout at her, but, it's no use. My eyes follow Xander as he makes his way down the hallway with Mr. Wilson closely behind. I can see his mouth watering. Disgusting.

I can feel the tears building in my eyes, but they're quickly burned away by the fiery rage consuming every fiber of my being. My fingers curl into my palm, forming a tight fist ready to be thrown as I watch on, unable to look away thanks to the Viper's tricks. I hate how much this is working. Everything Xander described to me unfolds right before my very eyes and I'm paralyzed. I can't stop it, not yet.

She's not ready to give up control. She wants me to break, to feel the need to send this vile human being straight to Hell where he belongs instead of breathing air he doesn't deserve to have in some enclosed space for the rest of his inhuman life. Three square meals a day, a chance to be let back into society with good behavior, to go somewhere else and do it all over again to someone else's child.

I watch him 'assist' my son with his aim and I'm ready to pounce, I'm ready to kill. But it's not enough. A flash and I'm in the classroom where Xander's being forced to perform for the extra credit he needs to pass in order to impress me with how well he's doing. Viper shoves a knife in my palm and finally allows me to pounce. Slashing, stabbing, and slicing until this Mr. Wilson is destroyed beyond all recognition. I can feel Viper's nod of approval as she allows me to return to reality. Now that I had been deemed ready after passing her test with flying colors.

17

Needless to say, Xander was taken out of school that week. My parents offered to show him and Nora around England where I grew up while Amelia and I sort out this fiasco. Although, she was working on the justice I was originally for while I do the Viper's bidding and stake out the pedophile's house for only two days, the shortest I have ever staked out a home before being sure I was ready to end his disgusting life. It was clearly the anger for what he's done to my boy, but I didn't care and Viper was pleased at her victory, ready to make an epic return to the killing game.

I admire Amelia's strength through all of this, going to the school to tell them about Mr. Wilson's heinous actions on our son, and who know what or how many other children he's done this things to. Innocent victims of a crime they know nothing about. While my wife was out doing that, Viper was putting together an extra special plan for this extra special prey. The return of the Viper is surely going to be an epic one.

Unfortunately for me, this little bugger locked his doors. Probably hiding some disgusting pornography, the prick. I'll have to come up with another way in and since I wasn't one for picking locks, I decide to play it cool. Nothing a little British charm can't do. I make my way to the front door on this fateful night and knock three times. When he finally opens the door, I give a sweet smile before plunging my knife into his side, forcing him backward in the moment of weakness where I catch him by surprise.

Following him in, I lock the door behind us before kicking him to the floor with a grunt. "Did you honestly think you could get away with it?!" I snarl at him, making my way over to deliver a powerful kick to his manhood through his sweats. A laugh erupts from my throat as I watch the pervert squirm in pain. He tries his best to crawl away, but I throw my daggers down just above each shoulder through the cloth of his shirt to keep him pinned. "MY son?! NOBODY does that to the Viper's child!" I bark, craving to kill him right then and there, but he hasn't suffered enough just yet. "You sodding little cockroach!!" I spit venom on his face as I tower above him. Stomping on the disgusting tool between his legs with as much force as I can possibly drive into it until he passes out from the pain. "Oh, no you don't."

I hiss, smacking him across the face multiple times to get him to wake back up and he begs for his life. It's like music to my ears. I've forgotten how much I loved this. So, I stab him right in the prick, slicing up the shaft. "Let's see how you like being violated, Mr. Wilson." My fingers grip his hair, allowing me to drag him into the kitchen. "Let's get creative now, shall we?" He tries to scream, but I put a stop to that real quick with a napkin in his mouth and tie one of the pieces of rope from my bag around his head to keep the napkin in; making him bite down before I slap a strip of duct tape over his mouth completely for added effect.

Then, I take a frying pan and set it on the stove, turning the burner on high before I start to beat him senseless. His blood staining my perfectly clean gloves. I can feel his bones breaking and it is oh, so satisfying. A few teeth knocked in, broken ribs, broken jaw and nose. He is ready for death, but the grim reaper just had to wait a tad bit longer to take this one down to the bad place.

When the bottom of the frying pan starts burning hot enough, I rip open his pants further and cut off his manhood, using the glowing pan to cauterize the wound. He blacks out from the pain and I take the time he's out to tie him to one of his nicer chairs from the dining room table, removing the duct tape from his mouth, untying the rope from around his head, and taking the napkin out of his mouth before I wake him right back up with the smelling salts. "Good morning, cockroach." I grin menacingly at him, holding up his detached little thing. "Aww, too soon?" I tilt my head, giving a smirk. Stuffing the bloodied pickle down his throat to choke on while I stab his flesh repeatedly all over his torso with the other hand.

His now lifeless body hunches forward, and I draw a simple V on his forehead in the blood taken from his chest. And that, children, is how the prodigal snake returns.

18

The next few days were filled with news reports covering the murder and Viper's return, the investigation opening up again to find out who exactly the Viper is. Too bad they'll never find out, not with what I have planned now. Viper wants to start a group where each member takes up the Viper name, killing for her. I had to admit that I liked the idea, made it less likely to get caught and easier to kill whomever I want. Lovely thought.

Also, several other children came forward about their own adventures with Mr. Wilson and what he did to them. It was baffling how much he actually got away with, but, he's gone now and it doesn't matter. Parents being interviewed about it praised Viper, thanking her for doing the right thing in avenging their children. You're welcome, but I didn't do it for you or your children. Just for me and mine. Doing my job.

I took off from work to be there for Xander and distract him from everything going on. Amelia joined me in England and we spend the better part of a month with my parents and the kids. Best family holiday ever, and a much needed one at that. Xander got his childhood back, and that's all that really mattered.

Although it was fun, the guilt of spilling blood again had been weighing down on me. Viper's back now, stronger than ever, and planning to create more of herself. I thought I would be strong enough to stop her, but, I'm utterly powerless and I don't know what to do. Should I tell Amelia? What would she think? Would she hate me? Thank me like the other parents have done? Send me to prison with James? Be terrified of me? I guess I had to get caught sooner or later, and she deserves the truth.

So, when we get home from our vacation, I wait a few days for us to settle back into our lives again before I decide to bring it up to her. I'm sitting up in our bed, watching her change into her pajamas that don't flatter her form well, but she likes them because they're comfortable and she still looks incredibly attractive to me. It's all in the face, really. That body is just icing on the cake, and oh, it is sweet. I smile as I admire her. Memories of our life together flash before my brown eyes, wanting to memorize the happiness on her features and remember the warm, comfortable feeling of unconditional love before I ruin it with my darkest secret of who I truly am.

My heart races as she makes her way over to her side of the bed when she's finished getting ready. I don't know if I'm prepared enough to say it, but, I need to get it out. So, I suck it up, clear my throat, open my mouth and speak. "Amelia, there's something I need to tell you…"

She looks over at me, concerned. My breathing increases in weight and my pause sends a vast amount of awful scenarios in her head, I can tell by the fear in her eyes. "What is it, babe? What's wrong?" She asks.

I close my eyes, exhaling slowly before finally giving her the answer. "I am the Viper."

19

She blinks a few times in confusion, tilting her head and it's obvious that she wants to laugh, but, doesn't want to feel like a bad wife for laughing because in her mind, it can't possibly be true. "But, Jade... The Viper is a man." She's smiling now, most likely thinking that I was just messing with her.

"No, darling... She isn't." I sigh, "It started that night at the Delta Nu party. I caught Jen being raped and from then, everything just went red. I killed... everyone." I swallow the lump in my throat at the memory. "First it started with her attacker. I broke an empty bottle and stabbed him until he died. Then, in just a fit of rage that nobody else bothered to help her, I took a kitchen knife and just--" I can't continue. The fear-stricken look of shock on Amelia's face is too much to handle, but I'm frozen in my spot in bed until she's able to tell me to leave. As she's processing the incredible explosive of information I had just dropped, I can see it in her eyes when it all just... clicks.

Then, she kisses me, much to my surprise. Her arms finding their way around my mid-section for a tight embrace and I find myself clinging to her thinking that this would be the last time. That the life we had built together is now over and there was nothing I could do about it. When she pulls away, she finally breaks the silence. "Wait, so... Xander is...?"

I nod, "Yes. I killed his family."

"And Mr. Wilson?" She asks.

"Yeaup. Me." I nod once more.

The questions continued for most of the night. She asked me how I did them, how I prepared. I told her about the classes and the voice. Oh, how I felt so relieved that this massive weight had been lifted from my shoulders from telling her. I really couldn't ask for anyone better than Amelia. She is absolutely perfect. So understanding, sympathetic, and kind. The love I felt for her only increased further and our bond now stronger than it has ever been. "I love you, Amelia." I tell her, pecking her lips just once. "I love you too."

Then my phone vibrates on the nightstand, abruptly ending our moment. "It's Jen." I tell her before reading the message she had sent, confused. "The news? Why?" Amelia shrugs at my question and proceeds to awaken the television from its slumber. Punching in the channel number for the local news station. "Convicted murderer, James Dawson, has escaped prison." The news anchor says just as the screen flickers over.

I lock eyes with my wife and am surprised by what I see. She's not afraid, no. Quite the opposite. She's actually confident and there's a twinkle in her eye. "Let's kill him." Amelia hisses. A chill runs down my spine and I can hear Viper laughing in the back of my head. "Armentum has begun."

<u>Acknowledgements</u>

There are a few people I'd like to thank for making this book possible. Each and every one of them have pushed me and supported me throughout the writing process, and I'm not sure if this story would've come to life without them.

Thank you, Nina, for all of your help and encouragement with all of your editing tips. Your belief in me and the bar you've set so high with your own publication are the reason I was able to achieve the goals I've set with this project. I hope I made you proud, Neeners!

Harley, without you founding the Knuckle Up crew, I never would have found the muse for this story; let alone stick with it until it was finished. I am forever grateful for you allowing me into the group with all of the amazing writers who have challenged me to better my own storytelling. This project exists because of you and I hope you can read this and see your own accomplishment as the first domino to fall.

Ava, I just want to thank you for your unconditional love and the undying support and encouragement to pursue this project and fight my way to the end. You are one of my best friends and I'm so glad to have you in my life.

To the rest of Knuckle Up, I just want to let you know that I love and appreciate all of you. Selina, Ivy, Jennay, and Lilith. Each and every one of you are phenomenal writers and I consider myself lucky to even know you and be surrounded by your talent. Thank you for your friendship and I can't wait to see what we cook up next!

About The Author

Born in Upstate New York and raised in the
Jersey Shore, A. B. Woods had a talent for
writing at a young age with a story to tell.
They currently still reside in New Jersey
with their dog, Luna, and work full-time to
pay the bills while working hard to make
their dreams come true.

46012648R00060

Made in the USA
Middletown, DE
20 July 2017